Nov. 12, 2016

Baby Bowers,

May you grow up
to be a strong
man of faith
who salts the world
with God's Truth.
May HE bless and
prosper you in
all ways.

In His Love,
Brenda
Woody

Miss Sugar and Mr. Salt

Written By Fred Marrs   Illustrated By Lori Duryea

Published by
Mother's House Publishing Inc.
Distinctive Books of Purity and Purpose
2814 E Woodmen Road
Colorado Springs CO 80920
719-266-0437 / 800-266-0999
info@mothershousepublishing.com
www.mothershousepublishing.com

Made in the United States of America.

ISBN 978-1-61888-134-2 hardcover

Just like sugar and spice
and everything nice,
between wishes and dreams,
it is just as it seems.
We were sipping' on Kool-Aid
and riding bikes in the rain,
exactly as He made us,
we became friends all the same.

It was fearless little boys, who met precious little girls,

wondering who made the mud
when all the questions arose.

"A Book for All Ages"
Author: Fred Marrs

*"A Child's Imagination is the
Art of Seeing the Invisible"*
Illustrator: Lori Duryea

DON'T BLAME ME.

IT'S NOT MY FAULT.

HOW WAS I TO KNOW...

THAT SHE WAS MADE OF SUGAR
AND HE WAS MADE OF SALT?

I SUPPOSE THAT SOMEONE SHOULD
HAVE WARNED THEM

BECAUSE THE WEATHERMAN HAD ALREADY SAID
THAT RAIN WAS ON THE WAY.

I LOOKED OUT THE PICTURE WINDOW.
IT WAS HARD FOR HIM TO STAND,
HE WIPED THE WATER OFF HIS LEGS,
AND IT WASHED AWAY HIS HANDS.

THE RAIN PELTED HER IN THE FACE
AND WASHED AWAY HER NOSE.

It poured and poured,

...and poured some more.

It turned the dirt to muddy.

I REFORMED
AND RESHAPED HIS HANDS
AND MADE HER TOES
IN A JIFFY.
I TRIED MY VERY BEST
ON THAT NOSE,
BUT IT WAS KINDA IFFY.

NOW THEY SAY SHE'S HAVING TROUBLE
LAYING FLAT UPON HER BED.
IT SEEMS I DID A DREADFUL THING.
I PUT HER NOSE ON THE BACK OF HER HEAD.

It was fearless little boys,
who met precious little girls,
with straight bangs and dark hair,
or blonde hair with curls.

Sometimes
we need a helping hand,
or we need to stand
on our own two feet.

With help given by others,
life can be really neat.

Author: *Fred Marrs*

Fred started writing stories in the 1980s. He progressed through college writing about his life experiences. Finally, he began writing poetry in 2007 with a child's interests at heart. Whether you're 6 or 66, 9 or 99, he'll make you laugh.

Education:
  Bachelor of Arts / Secondary Education
  Mid-America Bible College

Experience:
  Approx. 18-20 years working with students with various challenges, and unique abilities.

Illustrator: *Lori Duryea*

"As a youth, I admired how artists like Norman Rockwell and Larry Toschik could take a blank piece of paper and make it come to life with illustrations. As I grew older and began to draw as well, I learned to enjoy watching each stroke of my own pencil reveal further enriched features and more enhanced characters on the page before me. Over time, different aspects of art have revealed different passageways into my own imagination."

Education:
• Bachelor of Fine Arts / Major: Illustration and Design
• Master of Arts / Specialization: K-12 Art Education

Experience:
25 years Advertising, Design, Illustration, Teaching
10 years International / Local Adoption Ministry

ThreeStrands

18